T0308606

ALiCE'S ADVENTURES IN #WONDERLAND

BASED ON THE BOOK BY
LEWIS CARROLL

EDITED BY
PENNY FARTHING

ILLUSTRATED BY
BATS LANGLEY

woodhall press

NORWALK, CONNECTICUT

Woodhall Press, 81 Old Saugatuck Road, Norwalk, CT 06855
Woodhallpress.com
Distributed by INGRAM

Alice's Adventures in Wonderland first published in 1865

Through the Looking-Glass first published in 1872

Alice's Adventures under Ground first published in facsimile edition 1895 and
reproduced by permission of the British Library

Select passages published by Woodhall Press 2018
Illustration text copyright © 2018 Woodhall Press
Illustrations copyright © 2018 Bats Langley
Text design by Casey Shain

Library of Congress Cataloging-in-Publication Data available
ISBN (hard cover): 978-1-949116-10-6
ISBN (paperback): 978-0-9975437-6-6
ISBN (e-book): 978-0-9975437-7-3

Contents

To my friends and family,
and especially my husband,
who have all helped me
on my own wondrous journey.

—**Bats Langley**

CHAPTER I

Down the Rabbit-Hole

Alice
was
beginning
to get very tired
of sitting by her sister
on the bank, and of having
nothing to do: once or twice she
had peeped into the book her sister
was reading, but it had no pictures or con-
versations in it, "and what is the use of a book,"
thought Alice "without pictures or conversation?"

Liked by **HeartYourQueen** and **65 others**

AliceInsideWondergram What is the use of a #book without #pictures or #conversation? #nobars #noservice #currentmood #bored

. . . suddenly a White Rabbit with pink eyes ran close by her. There was nothing so VERY remarkable in that; nor did Alice think it so VERY much out of the way to hear the Rabbit say to itself,

"Oh dear! Oh dear! I shall be late!"

(when she thought it over afterwards, it occurred to her that she ought to have wondered at this, but at the time it all seemed quite natural); but when the Rabbit actually took a watch out of its waistcoat-pocket, and looked at it, and then hurried on, Alice started to her feet, for it flashed across her mind that she had never before seen a rabbit with either a waistcoat-pocket, or a watch to take out of it, and burning with curiosity, she ran across the field after it, and fortunately was just in time to see it pop down a large rabbit-hole under the hedge.

AliceInsideWondergram

Liked by **RabbitRaced4Time** and **148 others**

AliceInsideWondergram #Rabbit with a #pocketwatch #burningwithcuriosity Hey #whiterabbit #whatstherush and #notevenahello

AliceInsideWondergram  •••

Liked by **HeartYourQueen** and **422 others**

AliceInsideWondergram Oh #Welllllll #falling down
a very deep #well #thishappened #Ahhhh #OMG
#whatshappening #falling in the deep #sendhelp

In another moment down went Alice after it,
never once considering how in the world she
was to get out again. The rabbit-hole went
straight on like a tunnel for some way,
and then dipped suddenly down,
so suddenly that Alice had
not a moment to think
about stopping herself

before she found

herself falling

down a

v e r y

deep

well.

Alice was not a bit hurt, and she jumped up on to her feet in a moment: she looked up, but it was all dark overhead: before her was another long passage, and the White Rabbit was still in sight, hurrying down it.

There was not a moment to be lost: away went Alice like the wind, and was just in time to hear it say, as it turned a corner, "Oh my ears and whiskers, how late it's getting!"

She was close behind it when she turned the corner, but the Rabbit was no longer to be seen: she found herself in a long, low hall, which was lit up by a row of lamps hanging from from the roof.

There were doors all round the hall, but they were all locked; and when Alice had been all the way down one side and up the other, trying every door, she walked sadly down the middle, wondering how she was ever to get out again.

Suddenly she came upon a little three-legged table, all made of solid glass: there was nothing on it but a tiny golden key, and Alice's first idea was that this might belong to one of the doors of the hall; but, Alas!

Either the locks were too large, or the key was too small, but at any rate it would not open any of them.

AliceInsideWondergram   •••

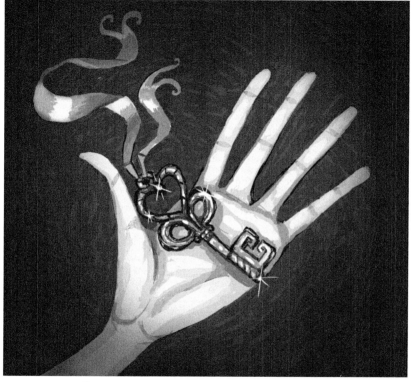

Liked by **RedQueenIsBest** and **292 others**

AliceInsideWondergram How will I ever get out again?
#ears and #whiskers #goldenkey #lockedout
#mustbeamonday #wakemewhenitsfriday #trapped

 **AliceInsideWondergram** ...

188 likes

AliceInsideWondergram Shutting up like a #telescope #nothing is #impossible

How she longed to get out of that dark hall, and wander about among those beds of bright flowers and cool fountains, but she could not even get her head through the doorway; "and even if my head *would* go through," thought poor Alice, "it would be of very little use without my shoulders. Oh, how I wish I could shut up like a telescope! I think I could, if I only know how to begin." For, you see, so many out-of-the-way things had happened lately, that Alice had begun to think that very few things indeed were really impossible.

11

There seemed
to be no use
in waiting by
the little door,
so she went
back to the table,
half hoping she might
find another key on it, or at any rate
a book of rules for shutting people up
like telescopes: this time she found
a little bottle on it, ("which certainly
was not here before," said Alice), and
round the neck of the bottle was a
paper label, with the words

"Drink Me"

beautifully printed on it in large
letters. It was all very well to say
"Drink me," but the wise little Alice
was not going to do *that* in a hurry.
"No, I'll look first," she said, "and see
whether it's marked '*poison*' or not.

AliceInsideWondergram •••

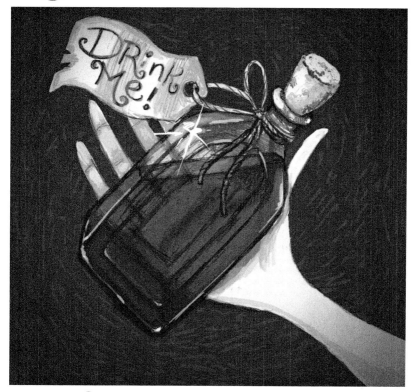

Liked by **RedQueenIsBest** and **1,226 others**

AliceInsideWondergram #DRINKME? Not that #thirsty
#thethirstisreal

View all 17 Comments

AliceInsideWondergram   ...

Liked by **TDum2** and **383 others**

AliceInsideWondergram Right size for going through the #littledoor into the lovely #garden #tiny #whocares #stillsmiling

However, this bottle was *not* marked "poison," so Alice ventured to taste it, and, finding it very nice (it had, in fact, a sort of mixed flavour of cherry-tart, custard, pine-apple, roast turkey, toffy, and hot buttered toast), she very soon finished it off.

"What a curious feeling!" said Alice. "I must be shutting up like a

telescope!"

And so it was indeed: she was now only ten inches high, and her face brightened up at the thought that she was now the right size for going through the little door into that lovely garden.

AliceInsideWondergram

Liked by **CallTheDutchess** and **275 others**

AliceInsideWondergram Don't mind if I do. #EATME
#cake #sogood #nothinghappening #whichway

Soon her eye fell on a little glass box that was
lying under the table: she opened it, and found in it
a very small cake, on which the words

"Eat Me"

were beautifully marked in currants.
"Well, I'll eat it," said Alice,
"and if it makes me grow larger, I can reach the key;
and if it makes me grow smaller, I can creep under the door;
so either way I'll get into the garden,
and I don't care which happens!" She ate a little bit,
and said anxiously to herself, "Which way? Which way?"
holding her hand on the top of her head
to feel which way it was growing,
and she was quite surprised to find that she
remained the same size: to be sure,
this generally happens when one eats cake,
but Alice had got so much into the way of
expecting nothing but out-of-the-way things to happen,
that il seemed quite dull and stupid
for life to go on in the common way.

CHAPTER II

The Pool of Tears

"Curiouser and curiouser!"

cried Alice (she was so
much surprised, that
for the moment she quite
forgot how to speak
good English);
"now I'm opening out
like the largest telescope
that ever was!
Good-bye, feet!"

AliceInsideWondergram ...

511 likes

AliceInsideWondergram Largest #telescope that ever was #Curiouser #curiouserest What's happening?! #isthisreal #goodbyefeet

 **AliceInsideWondergram** ...

Liked by **HeartYourQueen** and **716 others**

AliceInsideWondergram Big girls DO #cry
#sorrynotsorry #ithappens #letitout #tallgirlproblems

"Dear, dear!
How queer everything is today!
And yesterday things
went on just as usual.
I wonder if I've been
changed in the night?

Let me think: *was* I the same when I got up this morning?

I almost think I can remember
feeling a little different.
But if I'm not the same,
the next question is
'Who in the world am I?'
Ah, *that's* the great puzzle!

. . . she looked down at her hands, and was surprised to see that she had put on one of the Rabbit's little white kid-gloves while she was talking.

"How *can* I have done that?" she thought. "I must be growing small again."

She got up and went to the table to measure herself by it, and found that, as nearly as she could guess, she was now about two feet high, and was going on shrinking rapidly: she soon found out that the cause of this was the fan she was holding, and she dropped it hastily, just in time to save herself from shrinking altogether.

. . . in another moment, splash! she was up to her chin in salt water . . . However, she soon made out that she was in the pool of tears which she had wept when she was nine feet high.

"I wish I hadn't cried so much!" said Alice, as she swam about, trying to find her way out.

"I shall be punished for it now, I suppose, by being drowned in my own tears!"

AliceInsideWondergram ...

Liked by **WhiteQueenIsBetter** and **1,442 others**

AliceInsideWondergram #drowned in my own #tears
Swimming in #saltwater
View all 5 comments

Liked by **RabbitRaced4Time** and **316 others**

AliceInsideWondergram #walrus? #hippopotamus?
No, #mouse and he hates #cats and #dogs
#AHHHmouse #newperspectives #newfriends

Just then she heard something splashing about in the pool a little way off, and she swam nearer to make out what it was: at first she thought it must be a walrus or hippopotamus, but then she remembered how small she was now, and she soon made out that it was only a mouse, that had slipped in like herself.

. . . So she called softly after it, "Mouse dear! Do come back again, and we won't talk about cats or dogs either, if you don't like them!"

When the Mouse heard this, it turned round and swam slowly back to her: its face was quite pale (with passion, Alice thought), and it said in a low trembling voice,

"Let us get to the shore,
and then I'll tell you
my history, and you'll
understand why it is
I hate cats and dogs."

CHAPTER III

A Caucus-Race and a Long Tale

"Ahem!" said the Mouse with an important air,
"are you all ready?

This is the driest thing I know.

Silence all round,
if you please!
William the Conqueror,
whose cause was favored by the pope,
was soon submitted to by the English,
who wanted leaders,
and had been of late much accustomed to
usurpation and conquest.

Edwin and Morcar, the earls of Mercia and Northumbria–"

AliceInsideWondergram ...

Liked by **MadAboutHattering** and **691 others**

AliceInsideWondergram #yawn of the dead
View all 23 comments

 **AliceInsideWondergram** ...

Liked by **HeartYourQueen** and **2,489 others**

AliceInsideWondergram I thought #dodos were #extinct? #onlyathimble #myprecious

Alice had no idea what to do,
and in despair she put her hand in her pocket,
and pulled out a box of comfits,
(luckily the salt water had not got into it),
and handed them round as prizes.
There was exactly one a-piece all round.

"But she must have a prize herself, you know,"
said the Mouse.

"Of course,"
the Dodo replied very gravely.

"What else have you got in your pocket?"
he went on, turning to Alice.

"Only a thimble,"
said Alice sadly.

CHAPTER IV

The Rabbit Sends in a Little Bill

"I know *something* interesting is sure to happen" she said to herself, "whenever I eat or drink anything; so I'll just see what this bottle does."

. . . "It was much pleasanter at home," thought poor Alice, "when one wasn't always growing larger and smaller, and being ordered about by mice and rabbits. I almost wish I hadn't gone down that rabbit-hole—and yet—it's rather curious, you know, this sort of life! I do wonder what *can* have happened to me! When I used to read fairy tales, I fancied that kind of thing never happened, and now here I am in the middle of one! There ought to be a book written about me, that there ought! And when I grow up, I'll write one—but I'm grown up now," she added in a sorrowful tone: "at least there's no room to grow up any more *here*."

Liked by **TDLDee1** and **1,759 others**

AliceInsideWondergram Who wants to #write my #book? #notagain! My life is like #fiction.

View all 27 comments

AliceInsideWondergram   ...

Liked by **MadAboutHattering** and **726 others**

AliceInsideWondergram #theregoesbill #solong #cya
#buhbye

Then came a little pattering of feet on the stairs. Alice knew it was the Rabbit coming to look for her, and she trembled till she shook the house, quite forgetting that she was now about a thousand times larger as the Rabbit, and had no reason to be afraid of it.

. . . She waited for some time without hearing anything more: at last came a rumbling of little cart-wheels, and the sound of a good many voices all talking together: she made out the words: "Where's the other ladder?—Why, I hadn't to bring but one. Bill's got the other—Bill! Fetch it here, lad!"

. . . She drew her foot as far down the chimney as she could, and waited till she heard a little animal (she couldn't guess of what sort it was) scratching and scrambling about in the chimney close above her: then, saying to herself "This is Bill", she gave one sharp kick, and waited to see what would happen next.

The first thing she heard was a general chorus of

"There goes Bill!"

CHAPTER V

Advice from a Caterpillar

"Who are *you*?" said the Caterpillar.

This was not an encouraging opening for a conversation. Alice replied, rather shyly, "I–I hardly know, Sir, just at present– at least I know who I *was* when I got up this morning, but I think I must have been changed several times since then."

. . . In a minute or two the Caterpillar took the hookah out of its mouth, and yawned once or twice, and shook itself. Then it got down off the mushroom, and crawled away into the grass, merely remarking, as it went, "One side will make you grow taller, and the other side will make you grow shorter."

"One side of *what?* The other side of *what?*" thought Alice to herself.

"Of the mushroom," said the Caterpillar, just as if she had asked it aloud: and in another moment it was out of sight.

 **AliceInsideWondergram** ···

Liked by **WhiteQueenIsBetter** and **3,242 others**

AliceInsideWondergram Does #anyone know who I
#am? #whatishesmoking #isitlegal?
View all 48 comments

AliceInsideWondergram ...

Liked by **RedQueenIsBest** and **188 others**

AliceInsideWondergram I'm never sure what I'm going to eat, from one minute to another! #mushrooms #magical #puzzling

"How puzzling

all these changes are! I'm never sure what I'm going to be, from one minute to another! However, I've got back to my right size: the next thing is, to get into that beautiful garden—how *is* that to be done, I wonder?" As she said this, she came suddenly upon an open place, with a little house in it about four feet high.

"Whoever lives there," thought Alice, "it'll never do to come upon them *this* size: why, I should frighten them out of their wits!" So she began nibbling at the right-hand bit again, and did not venture to go near the house till she had brought herself down to nine inches again.

CHAPTER VI

Pig and Pepper

. . . "There's no sort of use in knocking," said the Footman, "and that for two reasons. First, because I'm on the same side of the door as you are: secondly, because they're making such a noise inside, no one could possibly hear you."

And certainly there *was* a most extraordinary noise going on within—a constant howling and sneezing, and every now and then a great crash, as if a dish or kettle had been broken to pieces.

. . . "How am I to get in?" asked Alice again, in a louder tone.

"*Are* you to get in at all?" said the Footman. "That's the first question, you know."

"Oh, there's no use in talking to him," said Alice desperately: "he's perfectly idiotic!" And she opened the door and went in.

AliceInsideWondergram •••

Liked by **MadAboutHattering** and **912 others**
AliceInsideWondergram Perfectly #idiotic #doorman
#doormat
View all 19 comments

AliceInsideWondergram •••

Liked by **CallTheDutchess** and **3,615 others**

AliceInsideWondergram I didn't know that #Cheshirecats always #grinned #themoreyouknow #catgotyourtongue

. . . "Please would you tell me," said Alice, a little timidly, for she was not quite sure whether it was good manners for her to speak first, "why your cat grins like that?"

"It's a Cheshire-Cat,"

said the Duchess,

"and that's why. Pig!"

She said the last word with such sudden violence that Alice quite jumped; but she saw in another moment that it was addressed to the baby, and not to her, so she took courage, and went on again:—"I didn't know that Cheshire cats always grinned; in fact, I didn't know that cats *could* grin."
"They all can," said the Duchess; ""and most of 'em do."
"I don't know of any that do," Alice said very politely, feeling quite pleased to have got into a conversation.

"You don't know much,"

said the Duchess;

"and that's a fact."

. . . The cook took the cauldron of soup off the fire, and at once set to work throwing everything within her reach at the Duchess and the baby— the fire-irons came first; then followed a shower of saucepans, plates, and dishes. The Duchess took no notice of them even when they hit her; and the baby was howling so much already, that it was quite impossible to say whether the blows hurt it or not.

. . . *"Here!* *You may nurse it a bit, if you like!"*

the Duchess said to Alice, flinging the baby at her as she spoke. "I must go and get ready to play croquet with the Queen," and she hurried out of the room.

. . . "If I don't take this child away with me," thought Alice, "they're sure to kill it in a day or two. Wouldn't it be murder to leave it behind?"

 **AliceInsideWondergram** •••

Liked by **RedQueenIsBest** and **505 others**

AliceInsideWondergram Save us from the #Duchess.
View all 8 comments

AliceInsideWondergram   •••

♡ ◯ ◁   ⊓

Liked by **CallTheDutchess** and **76 others**

AliceInsideWondergram #ugly #child but a
#handsome #pig

View all 16 comments

Alice was just beginning to think to herself, "Now, what am I to do with this creature, when I get home?" when it grunted again, so violently, that she looked down into its face in some alarm. This time there could be *no* mistake about it: it was neither more nor less than a pig, and she felt that it would be quite absurd for her to carry it any further.

So she set the little creature down, and felt quite relieved to see it trot away quietly into the wood.

"If it had grown up," she said to herself, "it would have made a dreadfully ugly child: but it makes rather a handsome pig, I think."

And she began thinking over other children she knew, who might do very well as pigs, and was just saying to herself, ""if one only knew the right way to change them—" when she was a little startled by seeing the Cheshire Cat sitting on a bough of a tree a few yards off.

"In *that* direction," the Cat said, waving its right paw round, "lives a Hatter: and in *that* direction," waving the other paw, "lives a March Hare. Visit either you like:

they're both mad."

"But I don't want to go among mad people," Alice remarked.

"Oh, you can't help that," said the Cat:

"we're all mad here. I'm mad. You're mad."

"How do you know I'm mad?" said Alice.

"You must be," said the Cat, "or you wouldn't have come here."

. . . it vanished quite slowly, beginning with the end of the tail, and ending with the grin, which remained some time after the rest of it had gone.

"Well! I've often seen a cat without a grin," thought Alice; "but a grin without a cat! It's the most curious thing I ever saw in my life!"

AliceInsideWondergram

Liked by **MadAboutHattering** and **4,397 others**

AliceInsideWondergram A #grin without a #cat is the most #curious thing I ever saw in my #life #allmadhere #mad #notme #maybealittle

CHAPTER VII

A Mad Tea-Party

There was a table set out under a tree in front of the house, and the March Hare and the Hatter were having tea at it: a Dormouse was sitting between them, fast asleep, and the other two were using it as a cushion, resting their elbows on it, and talking over its head. "Very uncomfortable for the Dormouse," thought Alice; "only as it's asleep, I suppose it doesn't mind."

The table was a large one, but the three were all crowded together at one corner of it: *"No room! No room!"* they cried out when they saw Alice coming.

"There's *plenty* of room!" said Alice indignantly, and she sat down in a large arm-chair at one end of the table.

AliceInsideWondergram ...

1,295 likes

AliceInsideWondergram #seatstaken? #nope #nothappening Does anyone around here do dishes?
View all 15 comments

The Hatter opened his eyes very wide on hearing this; but all he *said* was

"Why is a raven like a writing-desk?"

. . . The Dormouse shook its head impatiently, and said, without opening its eyes, "Of course, of course: just what I was going to remark myself."

"Have you guessed the riddle yet?" the Hatter said, turning to Alice again.

"No, I give it up," Alice replied. "What's the answer?"

"I haven't the slightest idea," said the Hatter.

Alice sighed wearily. "I think you might do something better with the time," she said, "than wasting it in asking riddles that have no answers."

"If you knew Time as well as I do," said the Hatter, "you wouldn't talk about wasting it. It's him."

AliceInsideWondergram ...

Liked by **RabbitRaced4Time** and **327 others**

AliceInsideWondergram Why is a #raven like a #writing-desk? #Namedropper #knowtimelikethepresent

AliceInsideWondergram

Liked by **WhiteQueenIsBetter** and **47 others**

AliceInsideWondergram #Did you ever see such a thing as a drawing of a #muchness? #rudeness #NoToBullying

View all 6 comments

The Dormouse had closed its eyes by this time, and was going off into a doze; but, on being pinched by the Hatter, it woke up again with a little shriek, and went on:

"—that begins with an M, such as mouse-traps, and the moon, and memory, and muchness—you know you say things are 'much of a muchness'—did you ever see such a thing as a drawing of a muchness!"

"Really, now you ask me," said Alice, very much confused, "I don't think—"

"Then you shouldn't talk," said the Hatter.

This piece of rudeness was more than Alice could bear: she got up in great disgust, and walked off; the Dormouse fell asleep instantly, and neither of the others took the least notice of her going, though she looked back once or twice, half hoping that they would call after her: the last time she saw them, they were trying to put the Dormouse into the teapot.

CHAPTER VIII

The Queen's Croquet Ground

First came ten soldiers carrying clubs; these were all shaped like the three gardeners, oblong and flat, with their hands and feet at the corners: next the ten courtiers; these were ornamented all over with diamonds, and walked two and two, as the soldiers did.

After these came the royal children; there were ten of them, and the little dears came jumping merrily along hand in hand, in couples: they were all ornamented with hearts.

Next came the guests, mostly Kings and Queens, and among them Alice recognized the White Rabbit: it was talking in a hurried nervous manner, smiling at everything that was said, and went by without noticing her.

Then followed the Knave of Hearts, carrying the King's crown on a crimson velvet cushion; and, last of all this grand procession, came **THE KING AND QUEEN OF HEARTS.**

 **AliceInsideWondergram** ···

♡ ◯ ◁   ⊓

Liked by **MadAboutHattering** and **33 others**

AliceInsideWondergram THE KING AND QUEEN OF
HEARTS #wonderland #royalty #1percenter

AliceInsideWondergram ...

Liked by **HeartYourQueen** and **218 others**

AliceInsideWondergram This place is a #zoo #croquet #gettoyourplaces

"Get to your places!"
shouted the Queen in a voice of thunder,
and people began running about in all directions,
tumbling up against each other:
however,
they got settled down in a minute or two,
and the game began.

Alice thought she had never seen
such a curious croquet-ground in her life;
it was all ridges and furrows;
the balls were live hedgehogs,
the mallets live flamingoes,
and the soldiers had to double themselves up
and to stand on their hands and feet,
to make the arches.

"How do you like the Queen?"

said the Cat in a low voice.

"Not at all,"

said Alice:

"she's so extremely—"

Just then she noticed that
the Queen was close behind her, listening:
so she went on,

"—likely to win, that it's hardly worth while finishing the game."

The Queen smiled and passed on.

AliceInsideWondergram ...

Liked by **HeartYourQueen** and **1,456 others**

AliceInsideWondergram #oops #ears everywhere
View all 56 comments

AliceInsideWondergram ...

Liked by **CallTheDutchess** and **111 others**

AliceInsideWondergram OFF WITH HIS HEAD!
@HeartYourQueen it's good to be the #queen
#cheshirecat #headhunting #rathernot

"Who *are* you talking to?" said the King, going up to Alice, and looking at the Cat's head with great curiosity.

"It's a friend of mine—a Cheshire Cat," said Alice: "allow me to introduce it."

"I don't like the look of it at all," said the King: "however, it may kiss my hand if it likes."

"I'd rather not," the Cat remarked.

. . . "Well, it must be removed," said the King very decidedly; and he called to the Queen, who was passing at the moment, "My dear! I wish you would have this cat removed!"

The Queen had only one way of settling all difficulties, great or small.

"Off with his head!"

she said, without even looking round.

AliceInsideWondergram
···

Liked by **MadAboutHattering** and **81 others**

AliceInsideWondergram #keepyourhead
View all 12 comments

The executioner's argument was,
that you couldn't cut off a head
unless there was a body to cut it off
from: that he had never had to do
such a thing before, and he wasn't
going to begin at *his* time of life.

The King's argument was,
that anything that had a head
could be beheaded, and that you
weren't to talk nonsense.

The Queen's argument was,
that if something wasn't done about
it in less than no time she'd have
everybody executed, all round.

(It was this last remark that had made the whole party look so
grave and anxious.) Alice could think of nothing else to say but

"It belongs to the Duchess:
you'd better ask *her* about it."

CHAPTER IX

The Mock Turtle's Story

The Gryphon sat up and rubbed its eyes: then it watched the Queen till she was out of sight: then it chuckled.

"What fun!" said the Gryphon, half to itself, half to Alice.

"What *is* the fun?" said Alice.

"Why, *she*," said the Gryphon.

"It's all her fancy, that: they never executes nobody, you know. Come on!"

. . . They had not gone far before they saw the Mock turtle in the distance, sitting sad and lonely on a little ledge of rock, and, as they came nearer, Alice could hear him sighing as if his heart would break. She pitied him deeply. "What is his sorrow?" she asked the Gryphon. And the Gryphon answered, very nearly in the same words as before, "It's all his fancy, that: he hasn't got no sorrow, you know. Come on!"

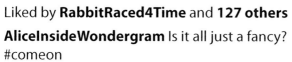

Liked by **RabbitRaced4Time** and **127 others**

AliceInsideWondergram Is it all just a fancy?
#comeon

"Once," said the Mock Turtle at last, with a deep sigh, "I was a real Turtle."

These words were followed by a very long silence, broken only by an occasional exclamation of "Hjckrrh!" from the Gryphon, and the constant heavy sobbing of the Mock Turtle. Alice was very nearly getting up and saying, "Thank you, Sir, for your interesting story," but she could not help thinking there *must* be more to come, so she sat still and said nothing.

"When we were little," the Mock Turtle went on at last, more calmly, though still sobbing a little now and then, "we went to school in the sea. The master was an old Turtle—we used to call him Tortoise—"

"Why did you call him Tortoise, if he wasn't one?" Alice asked.

"We called him Tortoise because he taught us," saidthe Mock Turtle angrily.

"Really you are very dull!"

AliceInsideWondergram   ...

642 likes

AliceInsideWondergram #rude #crymeariver
#alreadydid
View all 3 comments

CHAPTER X

The Lobster-Quadrille

"The lobsters!" shouted the Gryphon, with a bound into the air.

"—as far out to sea as you can—"

"Swim after them!" screamed the Gryphon.

"Turn a somersault in the sea!" cried the Mock Turtle, capering wildly about.

"Change lobsters again!" yelled the Gryphon at the top of its voice.

"Back to land again, and—that's all the first figure," said the Mock Turtle, suddenly dropping his voice; and the two creatures, who had been jumping about like mad things all this time, sat down again very sadly and quietly, and looked at Alice.

"It must be a very pretty dance," said Alice timidly.

 **AliceInsideWondergram** • • •

Liked by **HeartYourQueen** and **316 others**

AliceInsideWondergram It must be a very pretty dance. . . #confused #lobsterdance #movingon #selfie

CHAPTER XI

Who Stole the Tarts?

The twelve jurors were all writing very busily on slates.

"What are they doing?" Alice whispered to the Gryphon. "They ca'n't have anything to put down yet, before the trial's begun."

"They're putting down their names," the Gryphon whispered in reply, "for fear they should forget them before the end of the trial."

"Stupid things!" Alice began in a loud, indignant voice, but she stopped hastily, for the White Rabbit cried out, "Silence in the court!" and the King put on his spectacles and looked anxiously round, to make out who was talking.

Alice could see, as well as if she were looking over their shoulders, that all the jurors were writing down "stupid things!" on their slates, and she could even make out that one of them didn't know how to spell "stupid," and that he had to ask his neighbor to tell him.

AliceInsideWondergram •••

Liked by **WhiteQueenIsBetter** and **38 others**
AliceInsideWondergram Jury of #peers #stupidthings
#stewpid
View all 7 comments

 **AliceInsideWondergram** •••

Liked by **RabbitRaced4Time** and **147 others**

AliceInsideWondergram First witness! Hands off the
#tarts #nothankyou

"Herald, read the accusation!" said the King.
On this the White Rabbit blew three blasts on the trumpet,
and then unrolled the parchment-scroll,
and read as follows:—

"The Queen of Hearts,
she made some tarts,

All on a summer day:

The Knave of Hearts,
he stole those tarts

And took them quite away!"

"Consider your verdict," the King said to the jury.
"Not yet, not yet!" the Rabbit hastily interrupted.
"There's a great deal to come before that!"
"Call the first witness," said the King;
and the White Rabbit blew three blasts on the trumpet,
and called out "First Witness!"

"Well, at any rate, the Dormouse said—"the Hatter went on, looking anxiously round to see if he would deny it too; but the Dormouse denied nothing, being fast asleep.

"After that," continued the Hatter, "I cut some more bread-and-butter—"

"But what did the Dormouse say?" one of the jury asked.

"That I can't remember," said the Hatter.

"You *must* remember," remarked the King, "or I'll have you executed."

The miserable Hatter dropped his teacup and bread-and-butter, and went down on one knee. "I'm a poor man, your Majesty," he began.

"You're a *very* poor *speaker*," said the King.

AliceInsideWondergram ...

Liked by **MadAboutHattering** and **630 others**

AliceInsideWondergram What did the #Dormouse say? #karma for the Hatter

View all 37 comments

CHAPTER XII

Alice's Evidence

"Let the jury consider their verdict," the King said, for about the twentieth time that day.

"No, no!" said the Queen. "Sentence first—verdict afterwards."

"Stuff and nonsense!" said Alice loudly. "The idea of having the sentence first!"

"Hold your tongue!" said the Queen, turning purple.

"I won't!' said Alice.

"Off with her head!" the Queen shouted at the top of her voice. Nobody moved.

"Who cares for *you*?" said Alice, (she had grown to her full size by this time.) "

You're nothing but a pack of cards!"

...

Liked by **TDLDee1** and **289 others**

AliceInsideWondergram #stuff and #nonsense #nothingbutapackofcards #helpme

 **AliceInsideWondergram** •••

Liked by **RedQueenIsBest** and **471 others**

AliceInsideWondergram I don't want to #wake
#curious #dream #wonderland

"Oh, I've had such a curious dream!"

said Alice.
. . . So she
sat on, with
closed eyes,
and half
believed
herself in
Wonderland,
though she
knew she
had but to
open them
again, and
all would
change
to dull
reality—

79

THROUGH THE SMARTPHONE-GLASS AND WHAT ALICE FOUND THERE

CHAPTER I

Looking-Glass House

"Now, if you'll only attend, Kitty, and not talk so much, I'll tell you all my ideas about Looking-glass House. First, there's the room you can see through the glass—that's just the same as our drawing-room, only the things go the other way."

. . . "Let's pretend there's a way of getting through into it, somehow, Kitty. Let's pretend the glass has got all soft like gauze, so that we can get through. Why, it's turning into a sort of mist now, I declare! It'll be easy enough to get through—"

She was up on the chimney-piece while she said this, though she hardly knew how she had got there. And certainly the glass *was* beginning to melt away, just like a bright silvery mist.

AliceInsideWondergram •••

Liked by **HeartYourQueen** and **60 others**
AliceInsideWondergram Quiet #kitty and listen to my #ideas
View all 15 comments

 **AliceInsideWondergram** ...

Liked by **RabbitRaced4Time** and **14 others**

AliceInsideWondergram Who are you #grinning at?
#clock

View all 3 comments

Then she began looking about,
and noticed
that what could be seen
from the old room
was quite common and uninteresting,
but that all the rest
was as different as possible.

For instance,
the pictures on the wall
next the fire
seemed to be all alive,
and the very clock
on the chimney-piece
(you know you can only see the back of it
in the Looking-glass)
had got the
face of a little old man,
and grinned at her.

YKCOWЯƎᙠᙠAႱ

She puzzled over this for some time,
but at last a bright thought struck her.
"Why, it's a Looking-glass book, of course!
And if I hold it up to a glass,
the words will all go the right way again."
This was the poem that Alice read.

JABBERWOCKY

"Twas brillig, and the slithy toves
Did gyre and gimble in the wabe;
All mimsy were the borogoves,
And the mome raths outgrabe.
"Beware the Jabberwock, my son!
The jaws that bite, the claws that catch!
Beware the Jubjub bird, and shun
The frumious Bandersnatch!"

 **AliceInsideWondergram** ...

Liked by **TDum2** and **414 others**

AliceInsideWondergram # backwards #Mirrorwriting
#poetry #JABBERWOCKY #beware

Liked by **WhiteQueenIsBetter** and **171 others**

AliceInsideWondergram Who needs to #walk when you can #fly? #icanfly #happythoughts

"But oh!" thought Alice, suddenly jumping up, "if I don't make haste, I shall have to go back through the Looking-glass, before I've seen what the rest of the house is like!

Let's have a look at the garden first!"

She was out of the room in a moment, and ran down stairs—or, at least, it wasn't exactly running, but a new invention of hers for getting down stairs quickly and easily, as Alice said to herself. She just kept the tips of her fingers on the hand-rail, and floated gently down without even touching the stairs with her feet: then she floated on through the hall, and would have gone straight out at the door in the same way, if she hadn't caught hold of the door-post.

She was getting a little giddy with so much floating in the air, and was rather glad to find herself walking again in the natural way.

CHAPTER II

The Garden of Live Flowers

"O Tiger-lily," said Alice, addressing herself to one that was waving gracefully about in the wind, "I wish you could talk!"

"We can talk," said the Tiger-lily, "when there's anybody worth talking to."

Alice was so astonished that she couldn't speak for a minute: it quite seemed to take her breath away. At length, as the Tiger-Lily only went on waving about, she spoke again, in a timid voice—almost in a whisper.

"And can *all* the flowers talk?"

"As well as *you* can," said the Tiger-lily. "And a great deal louder."

 **AliceInsideWondergram** ...

Liked by **TheRealHumptyD** and **1,253 others**

AliceInsideWondergram #flowers can #talk
#snapdragonchat
View all 79 comments

AliceInsideWondergram · · ·

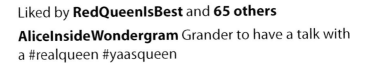
Liked by **RedQueenIsBest** and **65 others**
AliceInsideWondergram Grander to have a talk with
a #realqueen #yaasqueen

"She's coming!" cried the Larkspur.

"I hear her footstep, thump, thump, along the gravel-walk!"

Alice looked round eagerly and found that it was the Red Queen.

"She's grown a good deal!" was her first remark.

She had indeed: when Alice first found her in the ashes, she had been only three inches high—and here she was, half a head taller than Alice herself!

"It's the fresh air that does it," said the Rose: "wonderfully fine air it is, out here."

"I think I'll go and meet her," said Alice,

for, though the flowers were interesting enough, she felt that it would be far grander to have a talk with a real Queen.

"Where do you come from?" said the Red Queen.
"And where are you going?
Look up, speak nicely, and don't twiddle
your fingers all the time."
Alice attended to all these directions, and explained,
as well as she could, that she had

lost her way.

"I don't know what you mean by *your* way,"
said the Queen:
"all the ways here belong to—but why did you
come out here at all?"
she added in a kinder tone.

*"Curtsey while you're thinking
what to say. It saves time."*

AliceInsideWondergram   ...

Liked by **RedQueenIsBest** and **50 others**

AliceInsideWondergram #curtseying for #time #lost
#where do I go?

 **AliceInsideWondergram** ・・・

Liked by **RedQueenIsBest** and **467 others**

AliceInsideWondergram #EightSquare I will be a #Queen #goals #visionboard

For some minutes Alice stood without speaking, looking out in all directions over the country—and a most curious country it was.

. . . "I declare it's marked out

CHESSBOARD!"

Alice said at last.

"There ought to be some men moving about somewhere—and so there are!" she added in a tone of delight, and her heart began to beat quick with excitement as she went on.

"It's a great huge game of chess that's being played—all over the world—if this *is* the world at all, you know.

Oh, what fun it is!

How I *wish* I was one of them!

I wouldn't mind being a Pawn, if only I might join—though of course I should *like* to be a Queen, best."

She glanced rather shyly at the real Queen as she said this, but her companion only smiled pleasantly, and said "That's easily managed. You can be the White Queen's Pawn, if you like, as Lily's too young to play; and you're in the Second Square to begin with: when you get to the Eight Square you'll be a Queen—"

Just at this moment, somehow or other, they began to run.

CHAPTER III

Looking-Glass Insects

"Tickets, please!" said the Guard, putting his head in at the window. In a moment everybody was holding out a ticket: they were about the same size as the people, and quite seemed to fill the carriage.

"Now then! Show your ticket, child!" the Guard went on, looking angrily at Alice.

And a great many voices all said together ("like the chorus of a song," thought Alice) "Don't keep him waiting, child! *Why, his time is worth a thousand pounds a minute!*"

"I'm afraid I haven't got one," Alice said in a frightened tone: "there wasn't a ticket-office where I came from.

And again the chorus of voices went on. "There wasn't room for one where she came from. *The land there is worth a thousand pounds an inch!*"

AliceInsideWondergram

Liked by **MadAboutHattering** and **145 others**

AliceInsideWondergram #oops no #ticket

View all 16 comments

 **AliceInsideWondergram** ...

Liked by **TDLDee1** and **39 others**

AliceInsideWondergram Am I your #friend? What is #friendship?

View all 4 comments

The little voice sighed deeply.
It was *very* unhappy,
evidently,
and Alice would have said something
pitying to comfort it,
"if it would only sigh like other people!" she thought.
But this was such a wonderfully small sigh,
that she wouldn't have heard it at all,
if it hadn't come *quite* close to her ear.

The consequence of this
was that it tickled her ear very much,
and quite took off her thoughts
from the unhappiness of the poor little creature.

"I know you are a friend,"
the little voice went on:
"a dear friend, and an old friend.
And you won't hurt me,
though I am
an inscct."

The Horse,

who had put his head out of the window,
quietly drew it in and said "It's only a brook we have to jump over."
Everybody seemed satisfied with this,
though Alice felt a little nervous at the idea of trains jumping at all.
"However, it'll take us into the Fourth Square, that's some comfort!"
she said to herself. In another moment
she felt the carriage rise straight up into he air,
and in her fright she caught at the thing nearest to her hand,
which happened to be the Goat's beard.
But the beard seemed to melt away as she touched it,
and she found herself sitting quietly under a tree

—while the Gnat

(for that was the insect she had been talking to)
was balancing itself on a twig just over her head,
and fanning her with its wings.
. . ."—then you don't like *all* insects?" the Gnat went on,
as quietly as if nothing had happened.
"I like them when they can talk," Alice said.

"None of them ever talk, where I come from."

Liked by **TheRealHumptyD** and **64 others**

AliceInsideWondergram #trains jumping brooks and #insects that talk— #wonderland

View all 4 comments

AliceInsideWondergram •••

Liked by **TDLDee1** and **462 others**

AliceInsideWondergram TO Tweedledum's HOUSE or TO THE HOUSE OF Tweedledee. #decisionsdecisions #directions #twitterdee #twitterdum #wazeplease

"And now, which of these finger-posts
ought I to follow, I wonder?"

It was not a very difficult question to answer, as there
was only one road through the wood,
and the two finger-posts both pointed along it.

"I'll settle it," Alice said to herself,
"when the road divides and they point different ways."

But this did not seem likely to happen.
She went on and on, a long way, but, wherever
the road divided, there were sure
to be two finger-posts pointing the same way,
one marked

"TO *Tweedledum's* HOUSE"

and the other

"TO THE HOUSE
OF *Tweedledee.*"

CHAPTER IV

Tweedledum and Tweedledee

They were standing under a tree, each with an arm round the other's neck, and Alice knew which was which in a moment, because one of them had 'DUM' embroidered on his collar, and the other 'DEE.'

"I suppose they've each got 'TWEEDLE' round at the back of the collar," she said to herself.

They stood so still that she quite forgot they were alive, and she was just going round to see if the word 'TWEEDLE' was written at the back of each collar, when she was startled by a voice coming from the one marked 'DUM.'

"If you think we're wax-works," he said, "you ought to pay, you know. Wax-works weren't made to be looked at for nothing, Nohow!"

"Contrariwise," added the one marked 'DEE,' "if you think we're alive, you ought to speak."

Liked by **TDum2** and **1,516 others**

AliceInsideWondergram Are they alive? #contrariwise
#restingemojiface
View all 76 comments

AliceInsideWondergram ...

Liked by **WhiteQueenIsBetter** and **51 others**

AliceInsideWondergram That's not #weird
#getmeoutofhere #whichway #onlyemojiexpressions
#instasmiles #emojis

"I know what you're thinking about,"
said Tweedledum;

"but it isn't so, nohow."

"Contrariwise," continued Tweedledee,

"if it was so, it might be;
and if it were so, it would be
but as it isn't, it ain't.

That's logic."

"I was thinking," Alice said very politely,

"which is the best way out of this wood:
it's getting so dark.

Would you tell me, please?"

But the fat little men
only looked at each other
and grinned.

"Are there any lions or tigers about here?"
she asked timidly.

"It's only the Red King snoring," said Tweedledee. . . . "
And what do you think he's dreaming about?"

Alice said "Nobody can guess that."

"Why, about *you*!" Tweedledee exclaimed,
clapping his hands triumphantly.
"And if he left off dreaming about you,
where do you suppose you'd be?"

"Where I am now, of course," said Alice.

"Not you!" Tweedledee retorted contemptuously.
"You'd be nowhere. Why, you're only a sort of thing in his dream!"

"If that there King was to wake," added Tweedledum,
"you'd go out—bang!—just like a candle!"

"I shouldn't!" Alice exclaimed indignantly.
"Besides, if *I'm* only a sort of thing in his dream,

what are *you*, I should like to know?"

AliceInsideWondergram ...

Liked by **RedQueenIsBest** and **114 others**

AliceInsideWondergram Are we only someone else's #dream? #redking #mydream
View all 12 comments

CHAPTER V

Wool and Water

She caught the shawl as she spoke, and looked about for the owner: in another moment the White Queen came running wildly through the wood, with both arms stretched out wide, as if she were flying, and Alice very civilly went to meet her with the shawl.

. . . "I'm sure I'll take *you* with pleasure!" the Queen said. "Twopence a week, and jam every other day."

Alice couldn't help laughing, as she said, "I don't want you to hire *me*—and I don't care for jam."

"It's very good jam," said the Queen.

"Well, I don't want any *to-day,* at any rate."

"You couldn't have it if you *did* want it," the Queen said.

"The rule is, jam to-morrow and jam yesterday— but never jam to-day."

AliceInsideWondergram ...

Liked by **WhiteQueenIsBetter** and **160 others**

AliceInsideWondergram #jam #to-morrow and jam #yesterday but never jam #to-day #nothanks

AliceInsideWondergram   •••

♡   ○   ◁   ⊏⊐

Liked by **MadAboutHattering** and **56 others**

AliceInsideWondergram #believe as many as six
#impossible #things before #breakfast

"Nobody can do two things at once, you know.
Let's consider your age to begin with—how old are you?"

"I'm seven and a half, exactly."

"You needn't say 'exactually,'" the Queen remarked.
"I can believe it without that.
Now I'll give *you* something to believe.
I'm just one hundred and one, five months and a day."

"I ca'n't believe *that*!" said Alice.

"Ca'n't you?" the Queen said in a pitying tone.
"Try again: draw a long breath, and shut your eyes."

Alice laughed. "There's no use trying," she said:
"one *ca'n't* believe impossible things."

"I daresay you haven't had much practice," said the Queen.
"When I was your age,
I always did it for half-an-hour a day.
Why, sometimes

I've believed as many as
six impossible things
before breakfast. . ."

Liked by **WhiteQueenIsBetter** and **130 others**

AliceInsideWondergram #hmm

View all 16 comments

She looked at the Queen, who seemed to have suddenly wrapped herself up in wool.

Alice rubbed her eyes, and looked again.

She couldn't make out what had happened at all. Was she in a shop?

And was that really—was it really a sheep that was sitting on the other side of the counter?

Rub as she would, she could make nothing more of it: she was in a little dark shop, leaning with her elbows on the counter, and opposite to her was an old sheep, sitting in an arm-chair, knitting, and every now and then leaving off to look at her through a great pair of spectacles.

. . . So she went on, wondering more and more at every step, as everything turned into a tree the moment she came up to it, and she quite expected the *egg* to do the same.

CHAPTER VI

Humpty Dumpty

"What tremendously easy riddles you ask!" Humpty Dumpty growled out.

"Of course I don't think so! Why, if ever I *did* fall off—which there's no chance of—but *if* I did—"Here he pursed his lips and looked so solemn and grand that Alice could hardly help laughing.

"If I *did* fall," he went on, "*The King has promised me*—ah, you may turn pale, if you like!

You didn't think I was going to say that, did you?

The King has promised me—with his very own mouth—to—to—d"

"To send all his horses and all his men," Alice interrupted, rather unwisely.

 **AliceInsideWondergram**

Liked by **HeartYourQueen** and **817 others**
AliceInsideWondergram #humptydumpty sat on a
#wall and this is not going to end #well
View all 51 comments

Liked by **TheRealHumptyD** and **125 others**

AliceInsideWondergram #Loveyourself
View all 7 comments

"Now I declare that's too bad!" Humpty Dumpty cried, breaking into a sudden passion.

"You've been listening at doors—and behind trees—and sown chimneys—or you couldn't have known it!"

"I haven't, indeed!" Alice said very gently. "It's in a book."

"I shouldn't know you again if we did meet," Humpty Dumpty replied in a discontented tone, giving her one of his fingers to shake; "you're so exactly like other people."

"The face is what one goes by, generally," Alice remarked in a thoughtful tone.

"That's just what I complain of," said Humpty Dumpty.

"Your face is that same as everybody has—the two eyes, so—" (marking their places in the air with this thumb) "nose in the middle, mouth under.

It's always the same.

AliceInsideWondergram ...

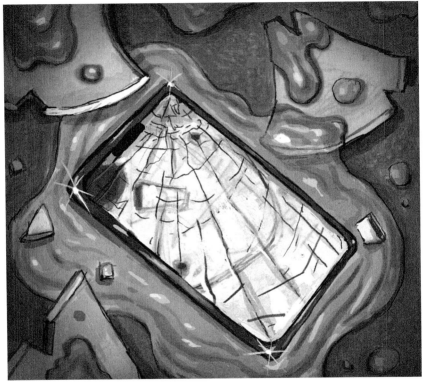

Liked by **HeartYourQueen** and **73 others**

AliceInsideWondergram #toldya #cracked
#crackedscreen
View all 16 comments

Now if you had the two eyes on the same side of the nose, for instance—or the mouth at the top—that would be some help."

"It wouldn't look nice," Alice objected.

But Humpty Dumpty only shut his eyes and said "Wait till you've tried."

Alice waited a minute to see if he would speak again, but, as he never opened his eyes or took any further notice of her, she said "Good-bye!" once more, and, getting no answer to this, she quietly walked away: but she couldn't help saying to herself, as she went, "Of all the unsatisfactory—" (she repeated this aloud, as it was a great comfort to have such a long word to say) "of all the unsatisfactory people I *ever* met—"

She never finished the sentence, for at this moment

a heavy crash shook the forest from end to end.

CHAPTER VII

The Lion and the Unicorn

Alice was very glad to get out of the wood into an open place, where she found the White King seated on the ground, busily writing in his memorandum-book.

. . . "I see nobody on the road," said Alice.

"I only wish *I* had such eyes," the King remarked in a fretful tone.

"To be able to see Nobody! And at that distance too!

Why, it's as much as *I* can do to see real people, by this light!"

. . . "Who are at it again?" she ventured to ask.

"Why, the Lion and the Unicorn, of course," said the King.

 **AliceInsideWondergram** •••

Liked by **WhiteQueenIsBetter** and **272 others**

AliceInsideWondergram Have you seen #nobody?
View all 27 comments

AliceInsideWondergram ...

Liked by **MadAboutHattering** and **1,267 others**
AliceInsideWondergram We're all #fabulous
#monsters #iloveunicorns #kingoftheforest #leolove
View all 101 comments

"This is a child!" Haigha replied eagerly, coming in front of Alice to introduce her, and spreading out both his hands towards her in an Anglo-Saxon attitude.

"We only found it to-day. It's as large as life, and twice as natural!"

"I always thought they were fabulous monsters!" said the Unicorn. "Is at alive?"

"It can talk," said Haigha, solemnly.

The Unicorn looked dreamily at Alice, and said "Talk, child."

Alice could not help her lips curling up into a smile as she began: "Do you know, I always thought Unicorns were fabulous monsters, too! I never saw one alive before!"

"Well, now that we have seen each other," said the Unicorn,

"if you'll believe in me, I'll believe in you. Is that a bargain?"

"Yes, if you like," said Alice.

. . . "Then hand round the plum-cake, Monster," the Lion said, lying down and putting his chin on his paws. "And sit down, both of you," (to the King and the Unicorn): "fair play with the cake, you know!"

CHAPTER VIII

"It's My Own Invention"

"How *can* you go on talking so quietly,
head downwards?" Alice asked,
as she dragged him out by the feet, and
laid him in a heap on the bank.

The Knight looked surprised at the question.

"What does it matter where my body
happens to be?" he said.

"My mind goes on working all the same.
In fact, the more head-downwards I am,
the more I keep inventing new things."

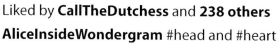

AliceInsideWondergram #head and #heart

Liked by **HeartYourQueen** and **121 others**

AliceInsideWondergram Long live the #queen!
#instafamous
View all 17 comments

. . . she watched the horse walking leisurely along the road,
and the Knight tumbling off,
first on one side and then on the other.
After the fourth or fifth tumble he reached the turn,
and then she waved her handkerchief to him,
and waited till he was out of sight.
"I hope it encouraged him,"
she said, as she turned to run down the hill:
"and now for the last brook, and to be a Queen!
How grand it sounds!"
A very few steps brought her to the edge of the brook.
"The Eighth Square at last!" she cried as she bounded across,
and threw herself down to rest on a lawn as soft as moss,
with little flower-beds dotted about it here and there.
"Oh, how glad I am to get here!
And what *is* this on my head?" she exclaimed in a tone of dismay,
as she put her hands up to something very heavy,
and fitted tight all round her head.
"But how *can* it have got there
without my knowing it?" she said to herself,
as she lifted it off,
and set it on her lap to make out what it could possibly be.
It was a golden crown.

CHAPTER IX

Queen Alice

"Well, this *is* grand!" said Alice.

"I never expected I should be a Queen so soon—and I'll
tell you what it is, your Majesty," she went on, in a severe tone
(she was always rather fond of scolding herself),
"it'll never do for you to be lolling about on the grass like that!

Queens have to be dignified, you know!"

. . . Everything was happening so oddly that she didn't feel
a bit surprised at finding the Red Queen and the White Queen
sitting close to her, one on each side: she would have
liked very much to ask them how they came there,
but she feared it would not be quite civil.

 **AliceInsideWondergram**   ...

Liked by **MadAboutHattering** and **318 others**

AliceInsideWondergram This is it? #dignifiedqueens
#selfiestick

View all 37 comments

At this moment the door
was flung open, and a shrill voice
was heard singing:—

"*To the Looking-Glass world it was Alice that said,*

'*I've a sceptre in hand,*
I've a crown on my head;

Let the Looking-Glass creatures, whatever they be,

Come and dine with the **Red Queen***,*
the **White Queen***, and* **me***.'*"

And hundreds of voices joined in the chorus:—

"*Then fill up the glasses as quick as you can,*

And sprinkle the table with buttons and bran:

Put cats in the coffee, and mice in the tea—

And welcome Queen Alice with
thirty-times-three!"

AliceInsideWondergram •••

Liked by **RedQueenIsBest** and **3,478 others**

AliceInsideWondergram Come and dine with the
#RedQueen, the #WhiteQueen, and #ME

 **AliceInsideWondergram** ...

Liked by **WhiteQueenIsBetter** and **99 others**

AliceInsideWondergram As for #you #insert #malevolent #laugh

"And as for *you*,"
she went on, turning fiercely upon the Red Queen,
who she considered
as the cause of all the mischief

—but the Queen was no longer at her side—

she had suddenly dwindled down to the size of a little doll,
and was now on the table,
merrily running round and round after her own shawl,
which was trailing behind her.

At any other time, Alice would have
felt surprised at this, but she was far too much
excited to be surprised at anything *now*.

"As for *you*," she repeated,
catching hold of the little creature
in the very act of jumping over a bottle which had
just lighted upon the table,

"I'll shake you into a kitten, that I will!"

CHAPTER X

Shaking

She took her off the table as she spoke, and shook her
backwards and forwards with all her might.
The Red Queen made no resistance whatever: only her
face grew very small, and her eyes got large and green: and still,
as Alice went on shaking her, she kept on growing shorter

—and **fatter**

—and softer

—and round
er

—and—

AliceInsideWondergram ...

Liked by **RabbitRaced4Time** and **67 others**

AliceInsideWondergram and. . . #fatter #softer
#rounder
View all 17 comments

CHAPTER XI

Waking

—and it really

was

a kitt🐱n,

after

all.

AliceInsideWondergram   ...

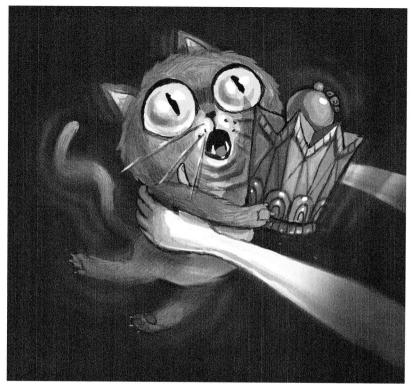

Liked by **CallTheDutchess** and **1,897 others**

AliceInsideWondergram Kitty! #felinelove
#catsofwondergram
View all 318 comments

CHAPTER XII

Which Dreamed It?

"Now, Kitty, let's consider who it was that dreamed it all.
This is a serious question, my dear, and you
should *not* go on licking your paw like that—
as if Dinah hadn't washed you this morning!
You see, Kitty, it *must* have been either me or the Red King.
He was part of my dream, of course—but then
I was part of his dream, too!
Was it the Red King, Kitty?
You were his wife, my dear, so you ought to know
—Oh, Kitty, *do* help to settle it! I'm sure your paw can wait!"
But the provoking kitten only began on the other paw,
and pretended it hadn't heard the question.

Which do *you* think it was?

AliceInsideWondergram ...

Liked by **HeartYourQueen** and **1,183 others**
AliceInsideWondergram Just a #dream?
View all 111 comments

Afterword

Alice has always held a special place in our hearts since we first saw the animated Disney version as children to when we read the adventures as told by Lewis Carroll. She has inspired countless fans over the years including our illustrator Bats Langley. Alice shaped our imaginations with the possibility of what if? What if we believed as many as *six impossible things* before breakfast? And what would Alice be like today? That question prompted this project, and we hope you have enjoyed the scenes we've selected to share with you our love of Alice. Please be sure to follow Alice @AliceInsideWondergram and all of her friends on their digital adventures.

Thank you for reading,
Bats Langley, Penny Farthing, Casey Shain, Woodhall Press

About the Editor

Penny Farthing "Who in the world am I? Ah, that's the great puzzle." Editor, author, and lover of all things Alice. For more information, please visit woodhallpress.com

About the Author

Lewis Carroll was actually a pen name! His real name was Charles Lutwidge Dodgson. He was born in 1832 and was a University of Oxford alum. Lewis, or Charles, taught mathematics and was known to be a renowned photographer. He wrote several other works but it was his two Alice adventure books that made him #famous. Both books, *Alice's Adventures in Wonderland* and *Through the Looking Glass*, are the basis for this book. He died in 1898.

About the Illustrator

Bats Langley is an artist and designer living in #NYC with his husband in the shadow of the Chelsea Hotel. He's excited to follow up the first book he illustrated, *Groggle's Monster Valentine*, with this latest project. A RISD alum, Mr. Langley is a regular contributor to *Spider*, *Ladybug* and *Cricket* magazines. Mr. Langley also shows his work in galleries and museums world wide. For more information, please visit www.batslangley.com. You can also find Bats Langley through the looking glass on Facebook or follow him down the rabbit hole on Twitter @batslangley and on Instagram @studiobatslangley.